THE INTERGALACTIC ADVENTURES OF
ZAKK RIDLEY
™
Ewan 2014
MARKOSIA

WRITTEN BY:
IAN SHARMAN & PETE ROGERS

ART BY:
EWAN MCLAUGHLIN

LETTERS BY:
IAN SHARMAN

FROM A STORY BY IAN SHARMAN

FOR MARKOSIA ENTERPRISES LTD

HARRY MARKOS
PUBLISHER AND
MANAGING PARTNER

GM JORDAN
SPECIAL PROJECTS
CO-ORDINATOR

ANNIKA EADE
MEDIA
MANAGER

ANDY BRIGGS
CREATIVE CONSULTANT

MEIRION JONES
MARKETING DIRECTOR

SARA WESTROP
COMMISSIONING EDITOR

IAN SHARMAN
EDITOR IN CHIEF

The Intergalactic Adventures of Zakk Ridley ™ & © 2014 Ian Sharman, Peter Rogers, Ewan McLaughlin &
Markosia Enterprises, Ltd. All Rights Reserved. Reproduction of any part of this work by any means without the
written permission of the publisher is expressly forbidden. Published by Markosia Enterprises, PO BOX 3477,
Barnet, Hertfordshire, EN5 9HN. FIRST PRINTING, November 2015. Harry Markos, Director.
ISBN: 978-1-909276-24-6

FOREWORD

Han Solo.

Mal Reynolds.

John Crichton.

Captain Harlock.

Cody Starbuck.

Add to that list:

Zakk Ridley.

We've a fascination with space pirates - there's something about people living outside the law: we'd run a mile if one turned up today, but set them in the past (Jack Sparrow, the most recognisable) or send them to the far future, we can imagine ourselves along for the ride, thumbing our noses at the stuffy restrictive authorities. For all their criminality, we want them to have some note of grace, an inherent, if reluctant nobility.

With Zakk Ridley, a put upon and maligned smuggler, his nobility walks beside him, in android form - Dan, a cybernetic Jiminy Cricket.

Ian, Pete and Ewan have, in this story, managed to create a universe that Zakk rebels against that isn't really that foreign - like all the best SF, it's a heartbeat in the future, not centuries hence. Not wanting to outline the plot, I'll just say that enough of this future world(s) rings uncomfortably close to society today.

Not to say this is some dark polemic, wagging it's finger at society's ills. Rather, like all the best pirate stories – it's *fun*. There's some great art in here, and some clever reversals. To say more would spoil your enjoyment - so, remember not to cross Lianna, and jump aboard the Mary J!

MIKE COLLINS

THE INTERGALACTIC ADVENTURES OF
ZAKK RIDLEY
#1
MARKOSIA
SHARMAN ROGERS McLAUGHLIN

JULY 12TH, 3086. THERON STATION, SECTOR 7.

Space is really quite sizable.

I mean... ...seriously... ...it's massive.

And... ...given just how IMMENSELY huge it really is, it's inevitable that SOME bits of it... ...are going to be a bit rubbish, really.

Sir, sensors are detecting one Spartelian and three humans within docking bay six. I'm downloading biological identifiers from Ethal Nuargi's identi-chip now.

One of these days, Dan, you'll actually download something useful...

...like the latest Ventures album or candid pics of Lindy Sanchez at the beach.

Theron Station is one such rubbish bit.

It's like the intergalactic equivalent of the services at Watford Gap...

...only the beans aren't as nice.

Sir, such activities would be morally dubious at best, and illegal at worst.
And we wouldn't want to do anything illegal, right?
MARY.J
BAY6

Exactly! Which is why I was pleased you accepted this job delivering legitimate medical supplies.
We don't want a repeat of that incident on Circarpous IV, after all.
I told you already, I have no idea how that girl got in there!

Zakk Ridley, it is being good to see you again, my friend.
I suspect you and I have very different definitions of the word "friend," Nuargi.
SUPPLIES

You are wounding me with your words!
But I am fearing it is true, men such as us cannot afford such luxuries as friendship.

Speak for yourself, we don't all roam the galaxy alone.
Ah, of course, gentlemen, I should introduce you to Zakk Ridley...
...and his long suffering tin sidekick.
His name is Dan.
Of course, I am forgetting that you humans like to name your things.
Even when you are winning them in a game of chance.
The money, Nuargi, do you have it?
You worry too much, Ridley.
AL SUPPLIES

See, monies! How could you ever doubt me?

Yeah, well, you won't mind if I count this...
Sir, I'm detecting several ships approaching the station...

It's a space station, Dan, of course there are ships approaching!
But, sir...

I'd love to say it's been a pleasure doing business with you, Nuargi...
Your pleasantries are being wasted on me, Ridley, and my clients are eager to leave.

Sir, I really must insist we...
MARY-J

INHABITANTS OF THERON STATION, DOCKING BAY SIX, THIS IS SECTOR PATROL 919.

ALL FOLLOWERS OF GOSHEN PREPARE TO SURRENDER.

YOUR SHIP AND ILLEGAL WEAPONS SHIPMENT WILL BE SEIZED AND YOU WILL BE TAKEN INTO CUSTODY.

Spit and space lanes, do they even bother training the police these days? Dan, patch me in to their COMS.

Opening a secure line now, sir.

Sector Patrol 919, this is Zakk Ridley, you might want to actually check your records for once. I'm carrying medical supplies and there aren't any Martyrs of Goshen here.

I mean, if there were they'd be...

...doing that?!

FOR GOSHEN!!

Sir...
Nuargi! You are dead!
Ridley, you are being many things, but a murderer you are not.
Maybe I've changed...
Zakk, Zakk, you are being my friend, I'm sure we can reach some kind of agreement here...
...which is mutually beneficial.
Now that would be telling. If you are getting me out of here safely, then we can discuss, no?
What could you possibly have to offer me right now?
No deal, Ethal.
Lianna taught me two things I'll never forget...
...and the second one was never trust a Spartelian!

How is Lianna?
Still scraping by on the Galactic Rim?
Why are you people being so afraid of embracing post-war galactic society?

Do you fear life in the P.G.A.F.P.*?
Do you fear Beckham?
Or is it civilisation itself you hide from?
*Pan Galactic Alliance of Free Planets.

Come on Dan, let's hit space, this one's not worth the oxygen.

Better hope the Sector Police are as understanding as I am, Nuargi.

Never fear, Dan, we'll soon be back in the void where we belong.
Hopefully not literally floating in it after the fighters I'm detecting have blown us up!
bleep boop
beep
click
click

We can outrun them.
Correction, sir, we can outrun the sector patrol ship, not the fighters.
We can outrun the fighters, we've done it before.
Oh no, not that, not again.
The last time we did that the ship ended up in dry dock for six weeks...
...you ruptured your spleen...
...and you still won't tell me how I got those stains in my...
THE

Dan, my good man, what is the use of us having a military grade C-Drive if we're afraid to use it?
Punch it!
SHOOOMM

LATER...
Have you found the Spartelian yet, Whatmore?
No, Commander Grail, the suspect appears to have absconded...
...and, uh, taken the evidence with him.

No ship, three dead Goshenites and no weapons.
I might as well hand in my badge now.

BAY 6
You can't blame yourself, sir...
...there was no way anyone could have guessed that heap of junk had a military grade C-Drive.
I don't blame myself, Whatmore, I blame you!
Let's just hope we can salvage something from this whole debacle when we get back to base.
MEDICAL SUPPLIES

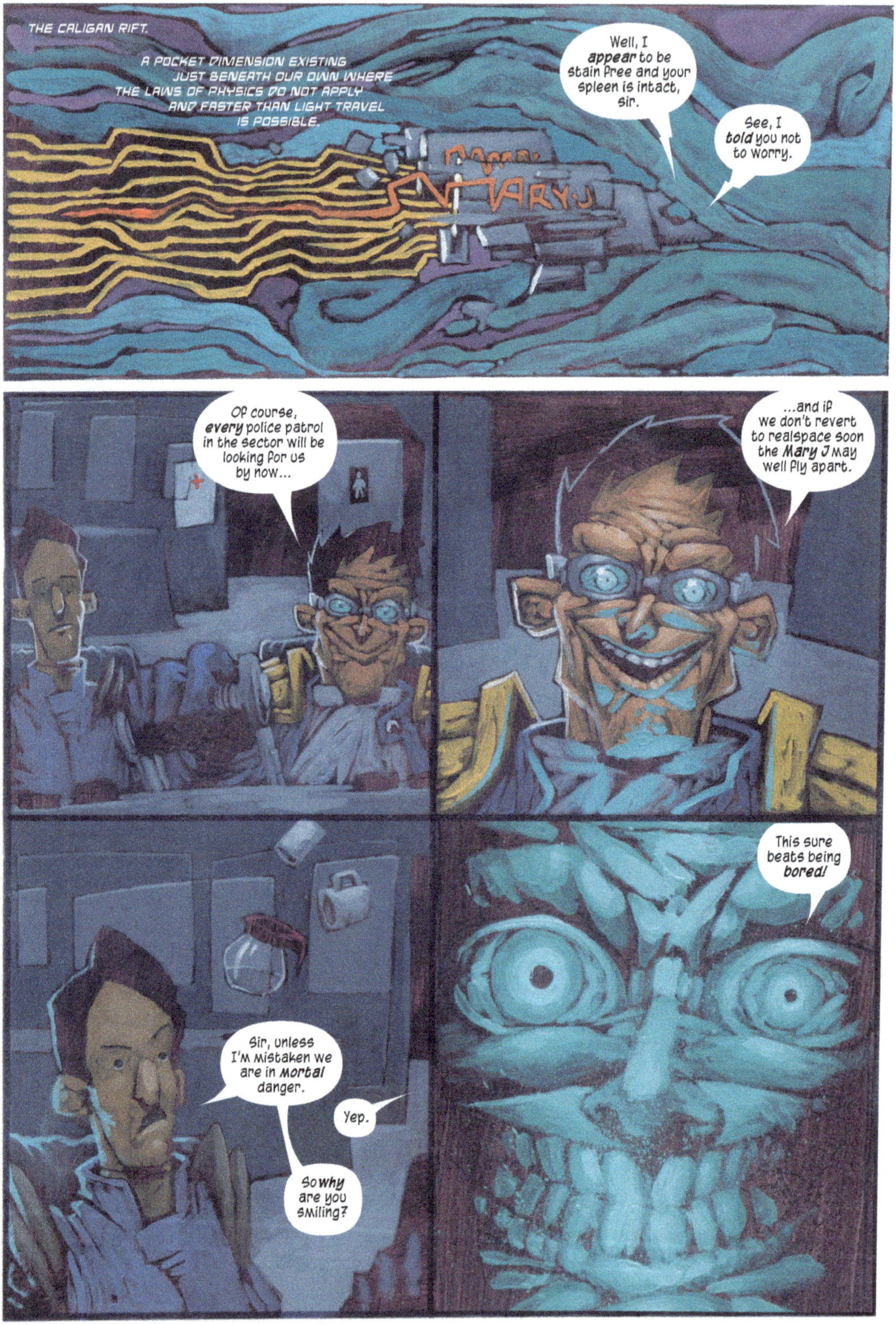

THE CALIGAN RIFT.
A POCKET DIMENSION EXISTING JUST BENEATH OUR OWN WHERE THE LAWS OF PHYSICS DO NOT APPLY AND FASTER THAN LIGHT TRAVEL IS POSSIBLE.
Well, I appear to be stain free and your spleen is intact, sir.
See, I told you not to worry.

Of course, every police patrol in the sector will be looking for us by now...

...and if we don't revert to realspace soon the Mary J may well fly apart.

Sir, unless I'm mistaken we are in mortal danger.
Yep.
So why are you smiling?

This sure beats being bored!

You are aware that records indicate that the last *fifteen* cases in which people were indicted for consorting with the Martys of Goshen...
...all concluded with the defendants receiving *termination* orders?

Rank *amateurs*, the lot of 'em!
I suppose you have a *plan*, sir?

We need a place to *land*.
Somewhere *safe*, ordinary looking, out of the way...
...but heavily guarded and with the necessary faciltiies to *fix* up the Mary J.

I'm entering those *variables* into the galactic database now, sir.
It may take a *while* for the system to find a match though.

No need, my *mechanical* first mate!
I know *just* the place...

SECTOR POLICE HEADQUARTERS.

We've been through this, sir, they had a military grade C-drive.
Whatmore, tell me how a beat up tramp freighter outruns state of the art fighters?!

This ship should have been decomissioned fifty years ago! What's a ship like this doing with a military grade C-drive?

We're, uh, still working on that, sir...
The media is going to have a field day with this...

There's no need for the exact nature of the situation to be public knowledge. I've contacted the quadrant spin specialist, sir.
Indeed. You're a good man, Whatmore.

Commander Grall, there's a priority call for you on channel one.
DIVISION 9
Tell them I'm busy.
But sir, it's the President.

ASTEROID SEVEN-EPSILON-PRIME, SUVEY SYSTEM.
At first glance it looks like a simple *mining operation* on the fringe of the galactic rim.
However, to those in the know, this is the main staging post for *Lianna T'Aren's* very exclusive delivery service.
Do you *really* think that Miss T'Aren will help us?
Some might call it *smuggling*...
...but *not* to Lianna's face.
Why *wouldn't* she? And don't call her "Miss T'Aren" to her face unless you want to be *dismantled* for spare parts.
Asteroid Seven-Epsilon-Prime, this is Captain Zakk Ridley of the light freighter Mary J requesting *permission* to land.
Zakk Ridley, you old *pirate*, what brings you to this misbegotten corner of the galaxy?
Maybe I just missed the *dulcet* tones of your voice, Lianna.
You always were a terrible *liar*, Ridley! Set the 'J down in bay *twelve* and then you can tell me what you want.

So, Zakk, what *trouble* is so bad that it's brought you running back to me?

I need a favour, Lianna.
Don't you always? Don't do much for a girl's ego, you know, just dropping by when you're in trouble.

It's the 'J, I've put her through hell and back today. Could do with some of your T.L.C.

You talking about your ship or yourself, Ridley?

Sir, would you like me to, um, wait in the ship for you?
No, no, Dan, that won't be necessary...
Oh my, Ridley, I do believe you're blushing!

So, are you going to help us? Or do I have to get out my little black book of ex's with starship repair bays?

Ok, boys...

You scratch MY back and I'll scratch yours.
...I'M going to need SOMETHING in return.
Look, whatever it is, we'll do it.

Anything?

Anything.

ELSEWHERE...
How do you want this to end?
What do you mean, how do I want this to end?
Alive or dead? Makes no odds to me, my fee don't change.
Dead. Definitely dead.

BACK ON ASTEROID SEVEN-EPSILON-PRIME.

You need me to get my hands dirty on the 'J, Ridley?
Between your repair crew and Dan and me, I think we've got it covered. That said, you do know her almost as well as me, so your input would be welcome.

My input would be welcome? When did Zakk Ridley become such a stiff?
Ma'am, my sensors indicate that Mr Ridley is no more or less stiff now than when I first encountered him.

Your robotic friend here is breaking my heart...
Go stow those supplies in the ship before you get me into any more trouble, will ya'?

So what is it that you want in return for all of this?
Patience, Zakk. Let's get the old girl back in the air before we start talking business.
SPACEWICHES

I acknowledge that some of the sanctions we put in place were intitially unpopular.
However, until this reign of terror which has been wrought upon us by the Martyrs of Goshen is brought to an end, we must remain ever vigilant.

NU-NU EARTH, KELLOTH SECTOR SPACEPORT.
PGAFP PRESIDENT TRAVIS BECKHAM GIVES AN IMPROMPTU PRESS CONFERENCE ON HIS RETURN TO THE SEAT OF GALACTIC GOVERNMENT.
When I was but a boy, my *father* told me something that is more true today than it ever was before.
"It is better to sacrifice *some* freedoms today, than to sacrifice *all* freedoms tomorrow."

OK, folks, we're *almost* done here.
The president does have a *busy* schedule but we do have time for one or two quick questions.
Yes, *Miss Zet'en*, go ahead.

Mister President, there are reports that a *Goshen* arms shipment was intercepted earlier today.
Surely this *proves* that your sanctions aren't working.

On the contrary, Miss Zet'en, that this shipment was intercepted *before* it could be used to terrorise citizens shows just how well...

Sorry folks, we need to call it a day.
The President has an... ah... urgent family matter to attend to.
Thank you all for your time and we'll update you further when it's appropriate.
GBC

Are you avoiding my question, Mister President?

Is the Goshen problem getting out of hand, Mister President?
Will you ever find Terrel, Mister President?

One person...
...how hard can it be to find one person?

MEANWHILE, BACK AT THE BASE...
That should do it.
I downloaded a new set of transponder codes while I was in there, so you shouldn't have any more problems with the sector police.
Thanks, Lianna.
You are clearly skilled in the mechanical arts, ma'am.
So, what exactly is our side of the bargain here?
I suppose I should put you out of your misery, Zakk.
It'll be just like old times, you and me working together again.
Seems you've got plenty of men here, Lianna, don't see what you'd be needing me for.
Oh, Zakk, I don't need you for anything...
...on the contrary, you need me, and that makes you mine.

I guess SOME things never change...
So, what's the job?

Nothing to write HOME about.
Just a SIMPLE pick up.

Right, just IN and out?
Should be no problem, so long as it's somewhere on the RIM...
I mean, you WOULDN'T send us to the galactic core...

You wouldn't send us to NU-NU EARTH, so it has to be...
ONDEBRON PRIME.

THE INTERGALACTIC ADVENTURES OF
ZAKK RALEY
#2

MARKOSIA

SHARMAN   ROGERS   McLAUGHLIN

Haha, I'm Zakk, Zakk Ridley! I'll kick ya' miserable butt into the middle o' the next millennium!

What on Nu-Earth are you doing?

Flying the ship...?
My goggles.
Give.

How far out are we anyway?
Not far, sir, I was just about to wake you. Did you have a good sleep?
No, I had a nightmare about a robot flying my ship...

SPACE PORT IIA-OP
I'll take her in, we can catch a shuttle down to *Reletta* from the space port. You'd better start getting the *stuff* Lianna gave us ready...

EARLIER...

I know you're no fan of the core systems, Zakk...
That's putting it mildly!
No way, no way, Lianna...

Ridley, you gave me your word...

The Lianna I know wouldn't hold that over me.

I have to concur with your evaluation, sir.
Our chances of success are minimal, at best forty three percent, according to my calculations.
Perhaps we should take our leave...

Now, wait just a minute...
...I didn't say that I couldn't do it, I just said that I wouldn't.

Really, Zakk? Maybe you're just turning chicken in your old age.
The Zakk I know would never back down from a challenge...

BWING
Yeah...
...we'll do it.

Less than forty three percent chance of success, sir...
Dan, were you manufactured with that stick up your ass?
Don't worry, I can give you some things that'll even the odds a little.

Okay, let me just grab a quick shower...
No time, Zakk, the clock's ticking on this already.

RELETTA.
CAPITAL OF ONDEBRON PRIME.
NOW.
FAZOO
POOT POOT

Who was she?
Who was who?
Lianna.

Are you programmed to ask awkward questions?
Her body temperature became elevated by two degrees each time she looked at you.

You can't just measure people's body temperature without asking!
I can't?

Stay calm and stick to the plan, Mr Thermometer.
Routine retina check, gentle beings.
Why but of course, my child.
You young men do such a wonderful service to the community.
Thank you, Father.
Everything seems to be in order here.
You can go about your business.
Move along.
Bless you, gentle beings, may the grace of God shine upon you...
What the hell was that?
I was just getting into character...
You'll be getting us thrown in prison if you keep that up!

My calculations indicate that, statistically speaking, we're unlikely to be so lucky if we're stopped again.
Statistically speaking you're a pain in the ass!
Lena

This is the place.
Local data feeds indicate that this building is designated for diplomatic aides and their support staff.

I smell money!
No wonder Lianna wanted this picked up urgently.

The apartment is registered to a Klaus Uberman, born just outside the Octagon Sector, forty nine years old...
Dan...
Shush.

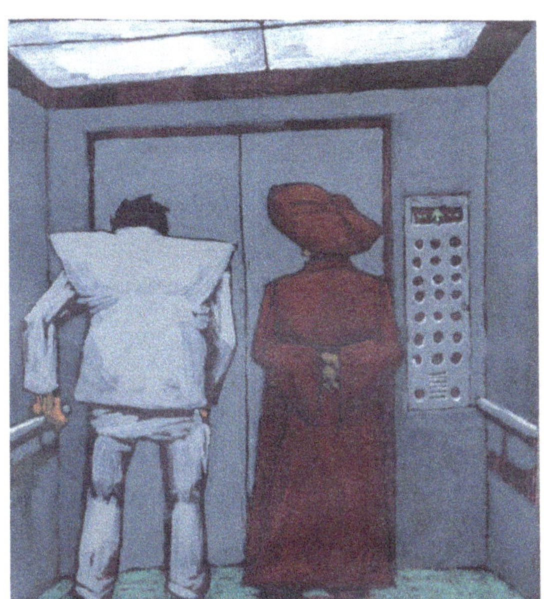

Is this it?
Oh, I'm sorry, would you like me to un-shush now?

What the hell is wrong with you? You've been acting up since we left Lianna's!

Do I need to book you in for a service?
No sir, my systems are running just fine.
Good, because I need you fully functional in here.
bling blong

Uh huh...
Well, hello...
Zakk Ridley? Lianna sent you?
I'm Kyouri Denan, and you're early.
You'd better come in while I get dressed.
Sir, your body temperature...
I think you're gonna need to bless me or something, Dan...
...because what I'm thinking is going to send me straight to hell!
Not now!
Ok boys, let's go!

Hangonaminute...
...you don't need to come with us. Just give us the package and we'll be on our merry way.
Didn't Lianna tell you? The package is me!
But... I...uh...
Uh uh, no way, no live cargo, not on MY ship.
Take it up with your boss, delivery boy. I need to get off this planet, now, and you're my ticket outta here.
-PLUT-
Women!
I heard that!

Don't you think your *friend* should be carrying those? It's not exactly a *priestly* activity...
Lianna, this is *not* what we agreed!

We never discussed the *nature* of the package.
Now get off the line before the authorities *trace* the call!
Okay, but we're *talking* about this when I get back.

You're *not* coming back here, Zakk, hasn't she told you?
Now, go, retina cloaks and disguises won't keep you off the *radar* for long.

Where is it *exactly* you think we're taking you?

That's for ME to know.
Well, I think I'M gonna need to know too if I'm flying us there...

Loose lips SINK ships, Ridley. You've got a MILITARY grade C-drive, yes?
Yes...
NEXT FLIGHT SPACE PORT 11

Good, then I'll tell you our destination once we're safely AWAY from prying ears in the Caligan Rift.

Sir! Sir!
I believe we MIGHT have a problem! The Sector Police channels are going HAYWIRE with chatter!

Thanks for the WARNING, my metal friend...
...but it looks like it MIGHT be a little too late!

Stop, or my MOM will shoot!
I just always wanted to say that...
What?!

Go! Get to the shuttle! NOW!

BLAM
Stop, or my MOM will shoot!
I just always wanted to say that...

Forget the bags! Run!!

Sorry about this, fellas...
...nothing personal, but I ain't ready to die today.
Aaargh!
PEW
Two men down, I repeat, two men down!
Suspect is approaching Shuttle Bay for Spaceport 11A.
Requesting immediate system lock down.
Fifteen minutes?
Dammit, that's too long...
BLAM
BLAM
BLAM

It's okay, it's not like you shot first...
This whole caper is going to ruin my reputation!
BLUJ.
CLOK1
Hold that shuttle!
CLOK1

Quick, sir, the shuttle's leaving!
SHTL
JALK
Close, dammit!
KSSSHHH

Pardon me, EXCUSE me, terribly sorry...
THIS is the plan? We just KEEP moving?
Will that WORK?

It will until we reach the END of the shuttle...
...then the best option is to take a hostage.

You are NOT taking a hostage!
I didn't say I was going to take a HOSTAGE. Did I SAY I was going to take a hostage?

NO GO
ZUG
Damn, the end of the line.
Looks like we've run out of SHUTTLE...
...and LUCK.

Stop or I'll shoot!
No you won't.
Explosive decompression... stuff like that...

You shot my friends.
They shot me first!
Plus, explosive decompression...

Oh, this is our stop!
Been nice talkin' with ya', but we've gotta go...

Ok, Dan, hit it...

SHHOOOMMM

So, let me guess, I'm taking you to Nu-Nu Earth?
How did you know?

It was the only way today could get any worse.

I've got a meeting with the GBC.
The Galactic Broadcasting Corporation?
Don't tell me all this is so you can audition For Factor: Z - Search For An Omni-Star?!

"If only..."

FIFTEEN YEARS AGO.

THE DENAN ESTATE.

Mr President! Congratulations on your landslide election win!

Why, thank you, Myo, your support is always very welcome.

Come on, Kyouri, time to go play upstairs.

Daddy has to work now, okay?

'Kay.

I trust you had a good journey, Mr Nadar.

Please, Myo...

...let's dispense with the *small* talk.
I didn't *risk* coming here just for a chat.
Let's get down to *business*, shall we?

Were you this *impatient* when working for my predecessor, Nadar?
I don't work *for* anyone, Beckham.
I work *with* them.

I've been following your career *closely*, Mr Nadar, I'm a big fan.
Your work during the *Rim Wars* was... exquisite...
You served the galaxy well as *Director* of Covert Military Operations.

Can the *flattery*, Beckham, I assume you're offering me a job.
A *new* job...
Quite. Something a little different, with some *unique* benefits.

Do go on...
Unlimited funds. Total immunity from prosecution.
Interested?
I'm listening...
Do you remember how loyal the people became during the war? How fear of a common enemy led them to obey every word of their government
What if you could bottle that loyalty?
How?
Simple, we give them something to be afraid of. Rally your men, I want you to terrify the electorate.
It's time for you to become public enemy number one.

Travis Beckham is behind The Martyrs of Goshen?
He's pals with Terrel Nadar?
Oh, please, you've been reading too many conspiracy holo-blogs.
Next you'll be telling me that Vita Narum is alive and well and living on the moons of Tenegrum!
But I was there, I heard it for myself...
You were a kid, you don't know what you heard. And I am not risking my neck for some conspiracy nut.
Dan, plot a course for the nearest system, Miss Denan is disembarking...

THE INTERGALACTIC ADVENTURES OF
ZAKK RIDLEY
#3
Ewan 2014
MARKOSIA
SHARMAN ROGERS McLAUGHLIN

Have you found somewhere to offload our cargo, Dan?
We can reach Tiberius in half a day.
You're seriously just going to dump me on some backwater world?
Oh no, I wouldn't do that.
Thank the Gods! You had me worried for a minute there.
We don't need to get to a planet, a space station will do.
You can't just put me off the ship! Lianna said you'd help.
Lianna says a lot of things.
About doing what's right?
About looking after number one.
The galaxy's a mess, don't you want to change things?
No, I like things just the way they are.

No elections?
Martial law?
You're happy with that?
I'm not arguing with you about this.
Because you know you'd lose.

Tell me you've found somewhere close to set her down, Dan?
A space station?
Perfect, I'm starving.
How does the Unaki System sound, sir?
There's a space station there at the intersection of three trade routes.
Miss Denan should be able to find a transport there...

Starving?
I just told you that the president is behind a major terrorist organisation...
...and that he's been using their attacks to manipulate the people of the galaxy...
...and all you care about is your stomach?

Look, it's nothing personal, I just cant risk everything...
...everything I have...
...on something you may or may not have heard a lifetime ago.
Then you're not the man Lianna said you were.

What can I say? I'm hungry.
Help me, Zakk Ridley, you're my only hope.

You got those coordinates yet, computer?
PROCESSING NOW, SIR.
COORDINATES WILL BE PLOTTED IN APPROXIMATELY TWENTY FOUR POINT ZERO ZERO FOUR ONE SECONDS.
Approximately, huh?
PRIORITY CALL COMING THROUGH FROM COMMANDER GRALL, SIR.
SHALL I ENABLE FLIGHT DECK HOLOCAMS?
Proceed.
Cregan, it's been a while, you've gone quiet on me.
Tell me you've got the target in your sights right now.
Grall, I'll contact you when the job's done.
I'm not one of your men, I don't report in.
bWOOP
Actually, I don't.
All I have is a name, and that's all I need.
You're being paid well enough to keep me informed.
You know how important this job is.

Now clear the *channel*, Grall...
...I need to get my *work* head on...
...because your precious little target should be coming into my *sights*...
...right about...

THE Laughing Goblin
Fresh Funk
...now!

Sporj
GUNS
WATER-FILLED GLASS BOWLS (WITH CREATURES IN)
You should be able to find supplies and safe passage to...
...well...
...wherever it is you wish to go, Miss Denan.
Oh, something smells good!
I don't... I don't...

Deep fried Alderbrian!
It's been years since I've had deep fried Alderbrian!
Aren't Alderbrian's a sentient species, sir?
All I know is that they taste good...

I suppose I'll be leaving then...

Sir, Miss Denan is taking her leave of us now.

Oh, really?
That's nice.
Now, what do you think, the Krytellian Blood Sausage or the Nega-Bird Eggs?

Well, goodbye, Mr Dan, the robot man.
Thank you for, you know, caring... at all...
Goodybe, Miss Denan, I do hope you'll be safe.

Really, sir, I've rarely known you to be so impolite!
Really?
Well, no, you're hardly known for your manners, but still...

Women and politics, Dan, women and politics!
It's a dangerous mix, and I ain't gettin' caught up in the middle of it, you hear?

But what if something happens to her, sir, how will you feel then...?

Who does he think he is, anyway?
Of all the arrogant, stuck up, half witted, scruffy looking...
Bioo woo woo woo woo!

Face it kid, you're lost.
And talking to yourself.
This is not a good combination.

Maybe down here...

Great! Just great!
I swear I'm going to kill Ridley if I ever see him again!
That's a mighty big if, kid...
DEAD

Did you really think they'd let you make it to Nu-Nu Earth?
One way or another, you were going to die, even if it meant blowing Ridley's ship out of the sky.

I'm almost disappointed you didn't give me an excuse to kill the insufferable idiot.

Oh, I don't know, he does have his good side...
...a certain charm...

Well, it's been nice chatting, but I'm on the clock here.
Time to die, Miss Denan...
BLAM.

What, no applause?
You just killed a man!
He was about to kill you! A simple thank you would be nice...
Thank you?
Thank you?!?!
None of this would have happened if you hadn't abandoned me in the first place!
Well, sure, but my underlying heart of gold won out in the end...
...and I did save your life.
Fine. Thank you. Can we get back to the ship now?

Oh, so you just *assume* that I'm letting you back on the ship.
Yes.

And *why*, might I ask, it that?

Because you *are*, don't deny it.
Well, *yes*...
Is nobody interested in hearing how I knew that Miss Denan was in *trouble* with the bounty hunter?

Yes...how *did* you know that I was in trouble?
PIZZ

Well, you see, it's really quite *simple*, as we were docking I noticed that there was a ship *following* us...

HANGAR 12
...and it was Cregan's ship and you knew he was a bounty hunter because you know EVERYTHING.
Yes, fascinating.
Ship now.

TWELVE
MARY
She might not look like much, but she's got...
Yes, yes, Ridley, we've all seen the ship before.
Come on, places to go, people to see...
I suspect a quip about putting you off the ship again is imminent, Miss Denan.

No, surely not, it would be too soon, don't you think?
Too soon, sir?

Sure.
I can't joke about putting her off the ship until she's actually back on it...
12

Yes, yes sir.
I understand sir, but...
No.
I understand.

CALL ENDED.
ENDCALL
blop
TEE-TEE

GRRRRAARGH!

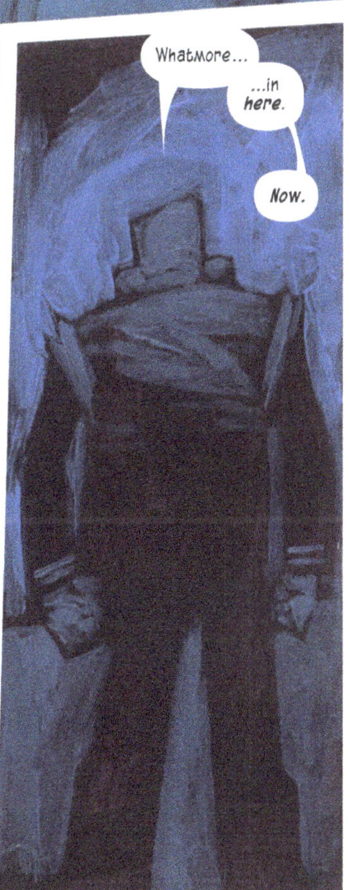

Whatmore...
...in here.
Now.

Nu-Nu Earth.
You will never find a more wretched hive...
Wait, no, not that, definitely not that.
Nu-Nu Earth is the thing planning laws were created to prevent. It's a vast, sprawling, never ending city on a million levels. There are parts of it that never see day light.
bLIMP

Heck, there are citizens of Nu-Nu Earth who are born, live out their entire lives and die without ever seeing the sun.
It's not a city, it's not a planet, it's a thing. A thing that exists by devouring people's lives.
In that respect it's not unlike Birmingham.

Hoods *up*, boys and girls.
Is this *really* necessary?
You wanna risk getting *scanned* by a hover cam and bringing Nu-Nu Earth SecureSec down on us?
Then be my *guest*, take your hood off!
Okay, Mr Tetchy, I was just *asking!*
TOOT TOOT
As you can see, preserving one's *anonymity* has somewhat driven the fashion on Nu-Nu Earth.
Enough people here have a good reason to not want to be *seen* that we won't stand out.
And here I was thinking this was the shining *heart* of the PGAFP.

Right, we need to find the GBC, which is no mean feat in a planetwide city.
I could just have Dan here hack the system, but we can't run the risk of that setting off any alarms.
I think I've just been insulted...
HELLO

It's seventeen klicks away, damn. Our best bet is to act like tourists and stick to public transport.
PANZY PUFF
LAST SAT-SUN

TOOT BRRR
HONK BROOOOM
VRRMM
BEEP
BEEP
I've ordered a taxi-pod, it should show up any...

...ah, here we are. Milady, your carriage awaits!
VWOOOo

So this is Nu-Nu Earth...
Yes, Miss Denan.
It's quite impressive.
You've seen one building, you've seen 'em all.
Were you always so cynical, Ridley?
I prefer to think of it as bein' a realist, kid. I'm less of a glass is half empty kinda' guy...
...and more of an if you don't leave my damn glass alone I'll shoot ya', kinda' guy.
And yet your best friend is the politest robot in the galaxy...

Why thank you, Miss Denan! And here we are, the GBC, that all went rather smoothly.

And this is where we say goodbye.
You're just leaving me here?
The deal was to deliver you, you're here.

Sir, are you sure it's wise to leave her on her own again?
Do you still doubt her story?
I don't care about her story, I ain't in this for her or her rebellion.
You keep telling yourself that, Zakk...

Not that I need an ageing space pirate with an inflated *ego* to help me do this. In fact, you'd *probably* be more of a hindrance.
And I'm talking to *myself* again...

Okay, play this *cool*, you're going to have to blag your way into here.

It's 3086...you'd have thought that humanity would have progressed to the point where I wouldn't have to *stoop* to this...

Uh... ma'am... miss...uh... can I...uh... can I *help* you?

Well I hope you can help me, you darling little man.
I'm here for an...ah... meeting with Mr Yalo.
I'll... I'll have to check the system for your appointment... ...um... what name will it be under?
Oh, I doubt you'll find our meeting on that lovely computer of yours... ...our liason is more, um, personal in nature.
Oh...oh... yes, ma'am... I mean miss... I mean... ...here's your securi-pass, head on up to level seven eighty two.
I'm, oh, sure Mr Yalo is expecting you...
Why aren't you just the most darling little man >smek<
And there goes my self respect...
ELEVATE

Come on, kid, you can do this.
Just focus, you've come this far, just one last step.

Pauly Yalo's an old friend, you know he can help you break this story.
Soon the whole galaxy will know the truth about Travis Beckham...

...and once everyone knows, I won't be in danger any more.
I hope...
P. YALO
VICE DEPUTY PRODUCTION CO-ORDINATOR G.B.C. NEWS

No...

YOU!
YOU DID THIS!

THE INTERGALACTIC ADVENTURES OF
ZAKK
RIDLEY
#4

MARKOSIA

SHARMAN   ROGERS   McLAUGHLIN
2014

Somewhere high above Nu-Nu Earth.

Commander Grall's Sector-Ship, The Illuminator speeds towards Nu-Nu Earth, armed with a full complement of turbo slazers and muon torpedos.

Whatmore, report!

Nu-Nu Earth, the very idea that any one man could rule over a world with so many inhibitants that, according to the latest census, its population is officially "I'm sorry, we've lost count," seems absurd.

Its deepest levels are less well charted than the galactic rim.

And yet one man not only claims dominion over this world, but all the worlds of the known galaxy.

We've tracked Ridley's ship, sir.
I don't like it, Whatmore, he should never have got this close.

It's worse than we thought, until recently Ridley's ship was docked in an upper level hangar. But as you can see here, he's on the move again.

But according to this, he's headed...

Captain, bodyslide on me to the co-ordinates Whatmore is feeding you now!
Now, man!

My, my, my, if it isn't little Kyouri Denan, haven't you filled out in all the *right* places?
It's a pity that you inherited your father's *foolishness*, but at least you have some of your mother's more alluring attributes...

What makes you think you have the right to talk about my family?
Because I owned them, just as I own everything else, including you.
This galaxy and everything in it belongs to me.
So you were a fool to think you could come to my TV network, on my planet, in my galaxy, to sell lies about me.
I wasn't selling anything, Beckham. You can't put a price on the truth.
Oh, I like that, I'll have to use it in one of my speeches...

How can you just stand there and laugh?
How can you be so insufferably smug when you've sent millions to their deaths?
You create fear and terror just to keep a firm grip on power!
My dear, I do not welcome power, I accept it as my burden.
And as I said on the Claude Mondial Show just last night...
"Every life lost in this war is a noble sacrifice on the altar of Freedom."
"No price is too high to pay for liberty."
But we're not free!
We live under twenty four hour surveillance, our every purchase is catalogued and recorded, and we have no say in our own government.
The price we've paid for liberty is liberty itself!
Nonsense!
The people of my galaxy are free!
They are at liberty to do as I please!

I am merely freedom's caretaker, looking after the fragile bird of liberty in this transitional phase.
In time those who refuse to conform to the majority will be weeded out.

We will honour them as they make the ultimate sacrifice for the greater good.
Eventually only the majority will remain, the good, the obedient, the pure.
And then we shall have peace.

You're insane. I see there's no hope for the galaxy with you in charge.
Just make it quick...

Such a tragic waste...

Mr President!
SHIING
PEW
eep!
What the...?!

What is the meaning of this interruption! How dare you?! I'll have your job for this, you jumped up little...

But, sir, Mr President, it's Zakk Ridley, you don't understand...
...we tracked him, his ship, he...
FISH FISH FISH FISH FISH FISH FISH
RUUMMMBLE

CRRSSSHHHH

Zakk?!

Argh!
Unh!
Ridley!
Ridley, you are nothing!
A nobody!
You've just signed your death warrant, Ridley!
And as for you, Miss Denan, your death will be slow, painful, and exceedingly pleasurable for me...

Aha...
No...
Ahh, my leg!
I can't feel my leg!
You're dead!
You're all dead!
SHHNK-

That's funny, I don't feel dead.
We've gotta make this quick, kid, Dan says we've got trouble inbound.
Well, well, Mr Ridley, it seems you have a few surprises left in you.
Dan reminded me that nobody signed for the delivery...

You think you're a hero, Ridley?
You know what a hero is?
Nothing but a fool I haven't killed yet.
This is my galaxy, your life will be short and full of pain from here on in...

Asteroid Seven-Epsilon-Prime, where Zakk Ridley's erstwhile employer takes some time to maintain her rag tag fleet of smuggler...um...I mean independent trading freighters.
Lianna T'Aren?
Yeah, tha's me, who wants ta' know?

You're coming with me, Miss T'Aren.
I don't think I am...

I have a Cat 12 Slaz Rifle here that begs to differ.
CLICK

Well, hello, Mr Slaz Rifle, I guess I'll be coming with you...

Back on Nu-Nu Earth...
So, while Mr Ridley was partaking of the local delicacies...
Can't this wait, Dan?
Miss Denan deserves an explanation, and I am quite capable of manoeuvring the ship whilst talking.
Tell you what, you talk, I'll fly.

As I was saying, as Zakk was eating I took some time to update my data banks by interfacing with the planetary network.
I ran a quick background check on the GBC while I was jacked in.
Six months ago Viridium Holdings bought a controlling share of the GBC.

Viridium is, of course, a subsidiary of Becktrochem, which is wholly owned by Travis Beckham.

If it wasn't for the money he's made from Becktrochem he wouldn't have been able to buy his way to the Presidency.
Precisely. This information caused me concern, so I did a network wide sweep for informantion on Pauly Yalo.

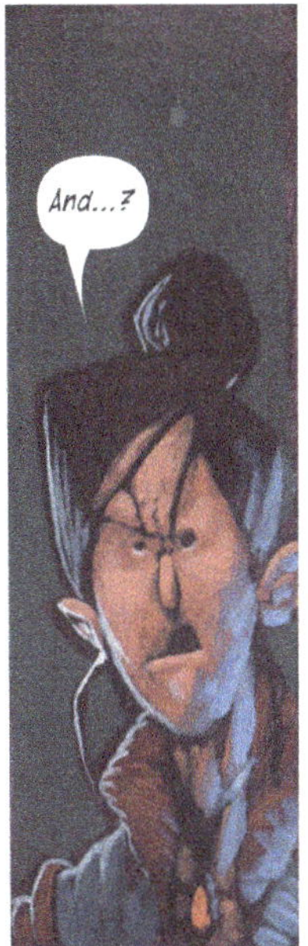

And...?

I found that a life insurance policy set to pay out a substantial sum was taken out for Mr Yalo just three days previously.
And the beneficiary was...
BECKTROCHEM!

Surely now you have to believe me?
It really does all add up, sir.

Sir?

Sir, are you quite all right?
Yes. Just more concerned with the fighters coming up on our tail than galactic politics!

Oh, great, fiery death from above?
Because today was going so smoothly...
Shush, we've got out of plenty of scrapes like this before...
We have?

We have. Sort of...
Did you just shush me?
Yes. Shush.

Mary J, you are to cease flight immediately and land on the nearest platform or be destroyed.
The President himself has issued an immediate termination order on all aboard your ship.
And what happens once we land?
So it's death or death? I choose cake!
PEW PEW Pew Pew PEW PEW Pew Pew

Can't you just fire up that fancy C-Drive of yours and get us out of here?

I'm afraid that would be quite impossible, Miss Denan.
We're still in atmosphere, firing up the C-Drive would probably ignite the air around the ship.
And we'd be consumed by the resultant fireball.
SWIV

Even if the atmosphere didn't ignite we're too close to the planet's gravity well.
We could cause a localised singularity and implode.
Please don't smile when you say that...

My apoligies, Miss, my anti-panic subroutines have kicked in.
I can't help but find everything pleasant and amusing.
It's either that or be forced to accept our impending doom.

Ridley, I will kill you if we die.

Oh, we're not dying...
We're not?
Oh no, we're having fun!

Dan, full stop.
In atmosphere?

Full stop.

What?
FWOOOOSHH
Where'd he go?

You'd think they never watch holo vids!

Yippe-ki-ay monkey Pudgers!
ZARK
ZARK
POW!

MARATHON
(WOOSH)

So what does the *talented* Mr Ridley have in mind now?
Well, I figure we're fugitives, the forces of the PGAFP won't *rest* until they have us in their evil clutches...

Why are you *grinning?*
Because it's so *exciting!*

Much as I *hate* to spoil your fun, sir... But I'm detecting a large number of *heavily* armed ships on our exit vector.

Oh, goodie, you know what *that* means...

Here we go *again...*

Punch it!
The stars blur into streaks of light as the Mary J's C-Drive opens a tear in the very fabric of space/time and leaps into the Caligan Rift...
...heading towards adventure.
SHOOOOM
The future awaits.
The end.
ewan 2014

ewan - 2014

ZAKK
RIDLEY
-The Further
Adventures

CWAHRGH

POW POW

blort

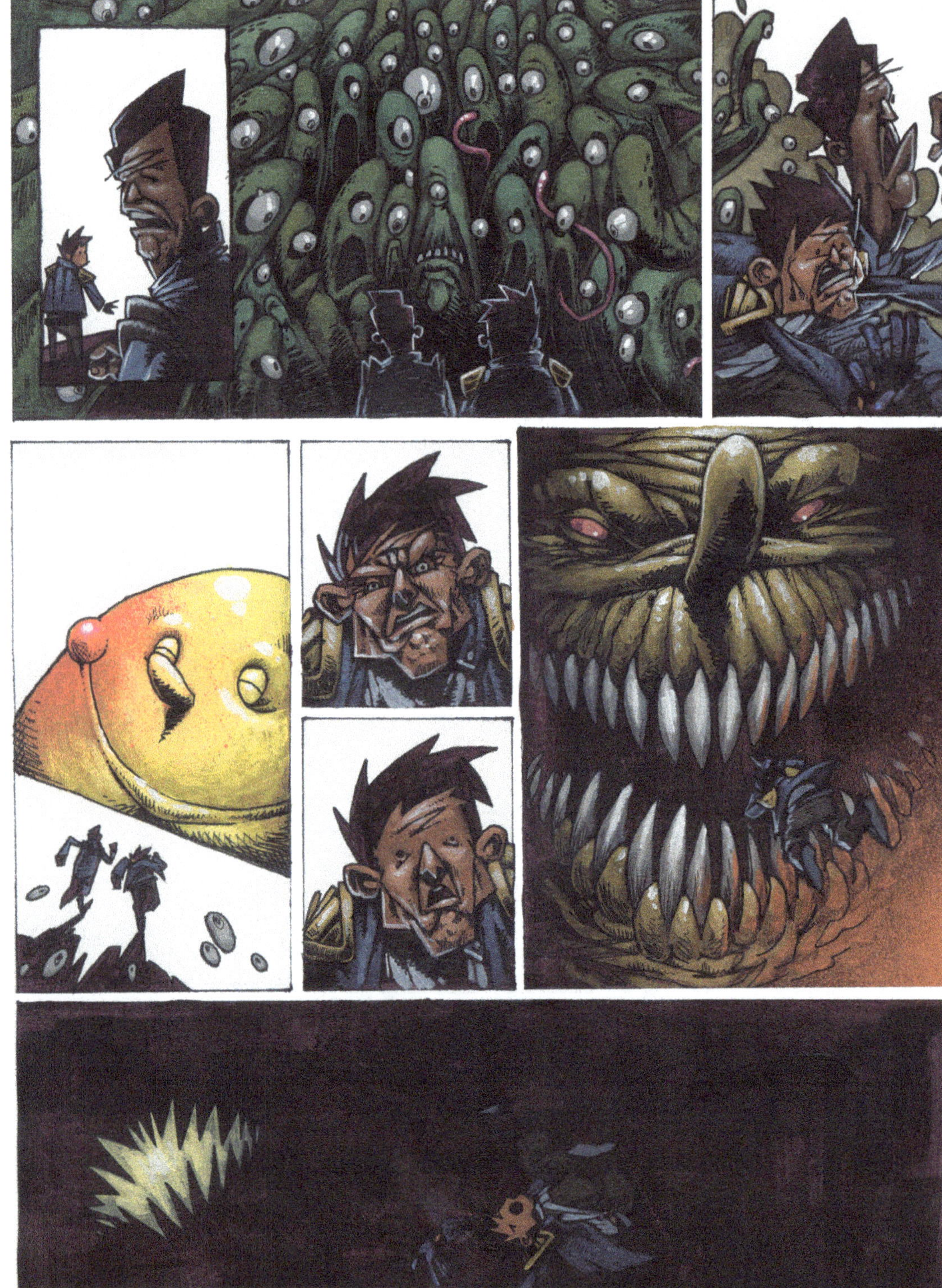

FWOMP
?
?

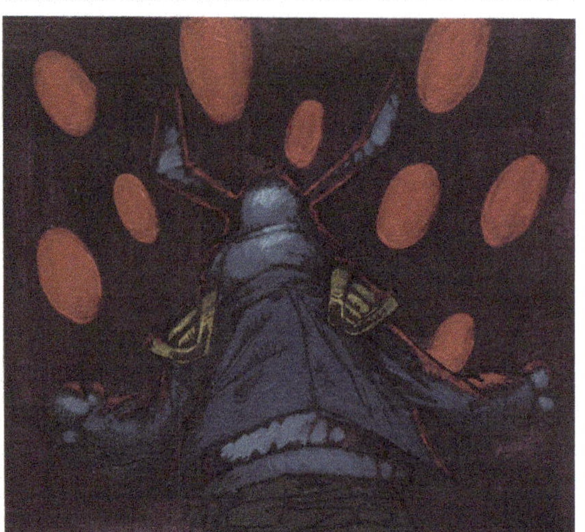

To be Continued...

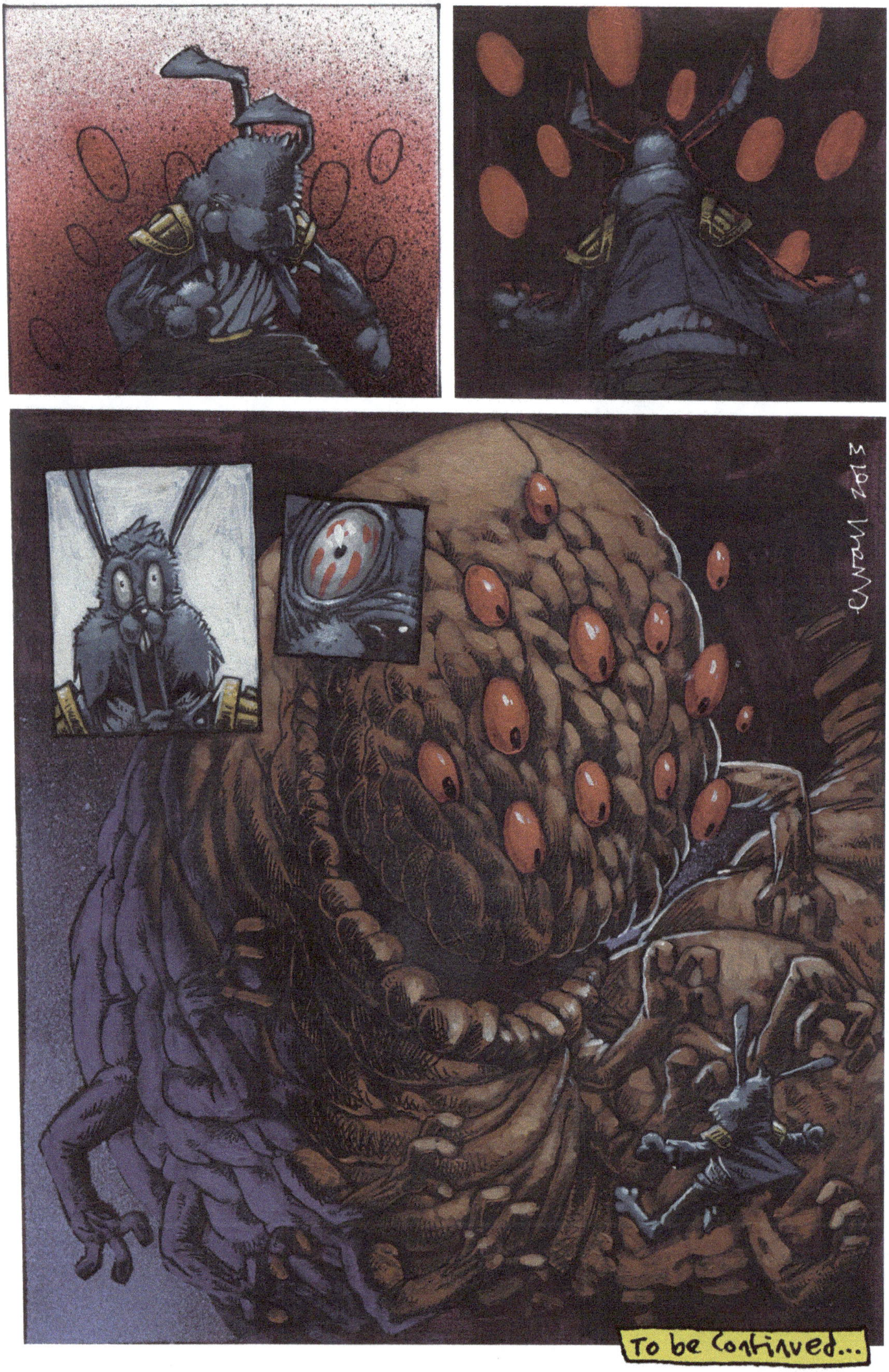

www.ingramcontent.com/pod-product-compliance
Lightning Source LLC
Chambersburg PA
CBHW041640010726
47507CB00011B/413